WITHDRAWN

Crab-boy
Cranc

Julie Rainsbury

Illustrated by Fran Evans

PONT READALONE

First Impression—2000
Second Impression—2001

ISBN 1 85902 835 7

© text: Julie Rainsbury
© illustrations: Fran Evans

This volume is published with the support of the
Arts Council of Wales.

Printed in Wales at
Gomer Press, Llandysul, Ceredigion SA44 4QL

Chapter 1

With my bad leg I shuffle, slightly sideways. It doesn't hurt, unless I'm really tired, but I can't mend the shuffle. Mam has always bought me the latest sports clothes and trainers because, she says, that's what all boys like to wear. But sports clothes never meant much because I couldn't run straight for football anyway. I was always different and my freckles and red hair didn't help. I just wanted to be like all the other boys.

Summers were the worst and summers were the best.

Summers were the worst because in class we always did the sea. I mean it—always, every year—the sea. There'd be tissue-paper fish on all the windows and a table piled with smelly seaweed, dead starfish, pebbles. There was always an old crab shell, pink and freckled like me. We'd get worksheets listing useful words for writing poems or stories about sea animals. That's when the whispers would start to go around—

'Cranc, Cranc, Cranc.'

At break, when we went out into the playground, the whispers became chanting, fierce as any football crowd—

'Cranc! Cranc! Cranc!'

Summers were the best because, at weekends, Mam and Dad and me went swimming in the sea. My leg works fine in the water, although my skin gets redder and more freckly in the sun on the beach.

Summer was even worse this year because of the school trip. Usually we get taken to Tenby, or for a tour of a lifeboat station or the Fishguard ferry. This year we went to the Aquarium and

a man there gave a talk. He made us touch sea anemones and a shark's skin, raspy as sandpaper. He lifted a giant crab out of a tank towards us. It was scarlet and spotty with terrible waving red bits. The whole class shrank back and a whisper went around the glass-tanked room—

'Cranc, Cranc, Cranc.'

It was a strange, fearful whisper—dark and dangerous, like water in a cave.

Mam just said,

'Take no notice.'

Dad just said,

'Call them names back.'

I tried to imagine it sometimes. I even picked
the names:

sharp and sneaky Steffan Siarc,

Wyn Walrus with his wonky teeth and
narrowed eyes,

slimy Siân Slefren Fôr, a jelly-fish full of sly,
stinging words.

Sometimes I half-closed my eyes and saw all
of us as sea-creatures, floating in and out between
the desks, a coral reef in the tissue-fished,
seaweed whiff, underwater world of our
classroom.

I could never say the names out loud, though.
That was me, cowardly Cai Cranc, always
nervous, always scuttling away to hide.

Chapter 2

Then this summer became the best one ever because Caradog came to our school. One day he was suddenly just there, a new boy up at the front of the class with our teacher, Mr Parry. Mr Parry's OK. A bit small and wet, but that's teachers for you. Mam says, when they go to Parents' Evening, he's got one of those damp handshakes, like a fish. Mr Parry Pysgodyn. Caradog blazed beside him, big and bold with hair even redder than mine. His hair wasn't only red—it bounced around his face in wild, corkscrew curls.

Usually new children look embarrassed or anxious or, at least, a little awkward. Caradog just looked as if he thought that he belonged, as if he'd been with us forever.

'Sit by Cai, Caradog,' Parry Pysgodyn said, pointing me out, and I was really pleased because no one ever wanted to sit by me.

'Cai will look after you and show you around.'

Some of the class sniggered and Siân said,

'Ugh, creepy Cai Cranc,' but softly so Parry Pysgodyn couldn't hear.

Caradog plonked himself down beside me and

beamed. He had one of those see-through, puffy, blow-up rucksacks in lime green. It was the sort of bag girls have but he didn't seem to care. Caradog didn't wear sports clothes either. He wore a turquoise T-shirt. It was plain, with no logo at all, and all baggy around the bottom. His shorts were a vibrant orange and came right down over his knees. With his clothes, bag and hair, Caradog was so bright that he almost seemed to glow. He was brighter than fruit gums or sunburn, brighter than lollipops or day-glo markers. He was a one-boy Bank-Holiday-beach colour. Worst of all, he wore sandals. Honestly. No socks or trainers, just brown leather sandals that might have belonged to someone's grand-dad or been worn by Noah in the Ark.

He must have noticed me staring because he nudged me in the ribs with his elbow, grinned and waggled his stubby, freckly toes. I grinned back and that's when we became best friends.

Chapter 3

Everyone liked Caradog. At first, Steffan would mock his red hair and mutter, 'Caradog Cimwch,' every time Caradog answered a question in class.

When Wyn saw us together in the playground, he'd yell, 'Cranc a Cimwch! Cranc a Cimwch!' while all his friends fell about laughing and joined in until the chanting rose and fell, rose and fell, like waves on a beach. So Caradog was Lobster-boy now! I would shiver and want to get away but Caradog would just smile, as if he enjoyed the joke.

Everything was always '*dim problem*' with Caradog. He never answered back. Caradog wasn't scared. Caradog really didn't care. He'd just get on with whatever he was doing.

It was the same when anyone mocked his clothes. Caradog would smile and shrug and never went home to nag his Mam to buy anything different. Caradog wasn't interested in what he looked like. He said clothes were just for being comfortable in—you know, not too hot, not too cold, not too tight, not too itchy.

Caradog seemed oblivious to any type of embarrassment.

He'd smile serenely if Parry Pysgodyn said his
work was wrong and simply . . .
   promised to try harder . . .
   or do it again . . .
   or make it tidier next time . . .
   or whatever.

Dim problem.

He didn't blush and stammer and wish the floor would open up to gulp him out of sight, the way I did.

Even when his Mam put little home-made cakes in his lunch box—you know, those ones you used to get at playgroup parties, babyish, girly ones with pink icing, flowery paper cases and hundreds and thousands on the top—Caradog didn't mind. He'd eat each one in two giant bites and offer around any spares.

So it wasn't long before everyone in the class liked Caradog. No one could help it. Caradog was smiley as sunshine, bright and bouncy as a beach ball, dazzling as a dolphin's leap, and Caradog was my best friend. We went everywhere together. Even our names went together.

'Cai and Caradog. Cai and Caradog.'

Sometimes I'd whisper them to myself, a comforting sleep-time shush, safe and gentle as low-tide on a shore.

Chapter 4

The only trouble was, Caradog turned out to be brilliant at football. I mean really brilliant. He was stunning wherever he played on the field. He could dart and dodge and dash to the attack, covering the whole length of the playground so fast that no one could catch him. The ball would behave as if it was glued to his sandalled feet until he blasted it into the goal. He hardly ever missed. Everyone would jump on him and hug him and yell, 'Ci-mwch! Ci-mwch!' until it sang in my head. It was a wild, exuberant sound, not scratchy and harsh and cross like *Cranc*.

He was great in defence, too, tackling all comers. But he was best of all as a goalie. Then he'd leap and catch corners that came at him like cannons or he'd dive onto the ball right in among all the thrashing trainers. He'd graze his knees and elbows but Caradog didn't care. He was fearless. All battered arms and legs, he covered any makeshift goal-mouth like a whirling octopus.

I always watched and cheered but I couldn't join in. My leg made me too slow for football. I was still clumsy Cai Cranc, hopeless as ever.

I preferred it when Caradog wasn't playing, when it was just the two of us being best friends.

I started to think that maybe winter would be the worst from now on. In winter, Caradog might want to join the local football club with Steffan and Wyn. He'd have boots and proper kit and training and away matches. Even if I went along to watch, I'd always be left out. Then Caradog might get fed up with me. Every time I hopped along the edge of the playground-pitch, cheering him on, I couldn't stop thinking about it.

Chapter 5

Then summer became the best of times again because our class was told that we were going to be taken to an adventure camp for the last week of term.

Once, I would have been nervous about going to camp. I would have worried about doing things wrong, being left out, being too slow, being lonely, being bullied. Now I had Caradog. I knew it would be OK.

I could tell Mam and Dad were surprised that I was so keen to go.

'Now, don't you take any nonsense,' said Dad. 'If they start, you call them names back.'

Mam frowned at him. 'Tell a teacher if you're worried about anything,' she said.

I've always wondered how grown-ups think you can get to a teacher if people are frightening you, watching your every move. Anyway, who would want to be called 'sneak' or 'cry baby' or 'teacher's pet' as well as 'Cranc'?

For once, I wasn't concerned.

'*Dim problem*,' I said. 'I'll be with Caradog.'

'Caradog, Caradog,' said Mam. 'We don't hear anything else these days.'

She smiled and folded tracksuits, pyjamas, shorts, T-shirts carefully into my sports bag, smoothing them flat on top of the underwear, swimming trunks, towels. I watched her impatiently. Why do mothers fuss and bother when it all rummages itself into a heap anyway, as soon as you try to take the first thing out?

'I'm told he's good at football,' said Dad.

My heart sank a little. Caradog would definitely be joining a team next season if even the grown-ups had heard he was good. Grown-ups are crazy about their sons playing football. Once last year, I'd heard Wyn and Steffan say the parents screamed so much and got so over-excited at a match that the ref. told them all to go and sit in their cars.

Dad tossed my wash bag into the air and headed it towards Mam's packing. It missed the sports bag and slid off the table onto the floor.

'Hopeless,' laughed Mam.

'Ah, well, swimming's our sport, isn't it, Cai?'

I nodded and smiled back at Dad and he gave me some money to buy crisps and sweets at the camp shop.

Chapter 6

At camp, everyone was too busy to think about playing football. It was great. The camp was perched right on the cliff-top. Fields fell away from it on all sides and then tumbled over the cliffs to the water. I loved being near the sea all day, watching its colours change from blue to green, turquoise, navy, indigo, silver, slate, black. I loved the weirdness of early morning sea mists and the way sunset made a shimmering path from the land to the horizon. It looked as if you could just step out onto the light and walk away into forever.

Every day there was something new to try. There were stables at the camp and groups of us were taken out to ride. A helper gave me a leg-up into the saddle and off I went with all the others. I was nervous at first, even though we were only walking the horses in single file around the edge of the field. My horse was called Bryn. He kept bending to tear mouthfuls of grass. Then he'd toss his head and make a sound like 'hrrrrummph'. I was worried that I might fall off. But then we were shown how to grip with our knees, how to steer and stop our horses with the reins, how to dig our heels into their warm flanks to make them go faster. We trotted in and out of markers, weaving patterns. I lay down across Bryn's back and felt him breathe beneath me. We cantered across a field and, even though I knew it was only a canter and not a gallop, we seemed to be flying. The sea glimmered far below and the sky was filled with the swoop of seabirds. We were caught between the water and the air. Wind whistled in my ears and Bryn's mane blew into

grey-white waves. I never got left behind when we were riding the horses. I didn't mind that the riding hat made my forehead itch. I even quite liked the hay and sweat and manure smell of the stables. Sometimes, when our group were not riding, we went on quad-bikes or on the plastic toboggans. My leg was no problem at all—horses, quads, toboggans—I could keep up with anyone.

On the second day, we went on the ski-slope for the first time. I'd never been on skis before

and my leg made me skew to one side and wobble and it was quite a struggle to get up again each time I fell. It didn't matter too much, though. There were plenty of other children who'd never skied before, so they were all falling over too. Some of them were crossing their skis and dropping their poles and bumping into each other and generally getting into as much of a muddle as me.

Even the ones, like Caradog, who swooshed confidently down from the top, sometimes crashed into the padded barriers or skidded over and grazed their arms on the roughness of the artificial slope. Caradog said it would be better and easier on real snow but it was still fun. We all hooted and cheered and laughed at each other and called each other names.

'Cranc, Cranc, Cai Cranc!' Steffan called out, as I shuffled sideways on my bottom, trying to stand up on my wonky leg after yet another fall. He was smiling at me. It was only a joke.

'Walrus!' I spluttered, as Wyn tried a fancy turn, fell and rolled into a great humped heap. He flailed his arms and legs about like useless flippers.

Wyn flopped over and dragged himself up with

his poles. He gave me a punch on the arm. It was one of those tappy sort of punches that you give when you're teasing a friend. I punched him back on the shoulder. We both giggled and edged off slowly towards the ski-lift to have another go.

Chapter 7

The best thing of all, for me, was the swimming pool. Although I'd done plenty of swimming with Mam and Dad in the sea and at the town pool, I'd never swum with lots of other children before.

In the first camp swimming session, we were divided into groups. I was in *Able Swimmers*. Caradog was in *Beginners*. I looked across at Caradog. It was the first time, apart from football, that we'd not done things together. He stood at the edge of the pool, pink and freckly and somehow smaller without his gaudy clothes. He was shivering, although it wasn't cold. His red curls quivered around his anxious face.

I loved swimming but Caradog hated every minute of it. He wasn't even really a beginner. Most of his group could swim with a float or armbands or do half a width of doggy-paddle. Caradog couldn't do anything at all. Caradog was frightened of water. No, it was worse than that. Caradog was absolutely terrified of water.

Caradog wouldn't jump into the pool or slide in from the side at the start of a session. He lowered himself slowly and reluctantly down the

steps. Everyone else had started by the time Caradog got into the pool.

Caradog didn't like putting his face in the water or lying back in it so that it lapped around his ears and he hated the splashing he had to put up with from everyone else's crawl kicks. Caradog spent most of each session holding on to the rail at the side. Sometimes he moved along the pool a short way and then back again. He always held the rail with both hands and never went out of his depth. If he really had to, Caradog walked around the shallow end holding a float and bobbing his shoulders up and down, pretending he could swim.

Caradog didn't moan or make a fuss, or do anything daft or dangerous, so the teachers didn't really take much notice of him. They were too busy. He never refused to take part, but his cheerful grin faded every time it was swimming. His mouth would go all thin and clenched and then he'd start to shiver.

Swimming was 'dim problem' for me. Swimming was wonderful. Swimming was wizard. Swimming was wicked. Mr Parry said I had a bit of a screw kick in breast stroke and that was probably down to my leg but, in crawl and backstroke and butterfly, I was unbeatable. I'd never realised I was so fast. I'd never realised I could out-swim all the other boys.

'We'll have to call you Cai Pysgodyn,' said Mr Parry, not realising that it was his own name. Mr Parry taught me a tumble turn and a racing dive. Mr Parry said he'd put me in the school team, next time there was a gala, and that I ought to join the swimming club in town.

When we got dry in the changing room, I'd ask Caradog if he was OK.

'*Dim problem*,' Caradog would say, but his smile looked a bit lop-sided. He never mucked about with us other boys after swimming. He always got changed and outside as quickly as possible. He said the smell of chlorine made him feel sick.

Chapter 8

The worst thing of all, for me, were the walks. Sometimes we were taken for walks inland along the lanes. Sometimes we were taken on the coast path and then down to the seaside village nearby. Whichever way we went, it was hills. If it wasn't hills on the way out, it was hills on the way back. Often it was hills both ways, up and down, up and down, like a switchback you had to walk, not ride. Hills make my leg ache. Hills make me shuffle more. Hills make me slower than slow. I was always falling behind. Caradog would wait

and walk with me. Caradog and I were always way behind. We were always last back. Once Mr Parry sent the mini-bus to pick us up. It was embarrassing.

When we went on the coast path, it was rougher but at least I got rests. Parry Pysgodyn would stop at the display boards that had been set up at intervals along the path. He'd read out the information on them to us—stuff about local birds and sea-animals and plants. I could sit down on the grass and recover while he told us about gulls and buzzards, dolphins and seals, gorse and thrift. The girls would plait long grasses and

31

gossip. The boys would scuff their trainers in the dust and throw stones out towards the sea. Now and again, Parry Pysgodyn would break off and tell someone to get away from the cliff edge.

It was good to look down on the sea from the cliff-top. A headland jutted out to the left below us. Sometimes the sea was different on each side of the headland—calm as a sheet of glass on one side, choppy on the other or deep sea-green on one side and a clear, bright blue on the other. The sea was strange and changeable. It could chant or shout or sing or sigh according to its mood. Its voice could be fierce as a threat or soft, as if it whispered your name. One day, the afternoon sun splashed stepping stones of light across its shifting surface. I felt I could step from one to another all the way to the dark-blue smudge of horizon.

I asked Caradog if he felt the same. Caradog stood up and adjusted the straps of his lime green rucksack.

'Water's tricky enough at the best of times,' said Caradog, 'without dreaming of balancing on sunshine.'

Caradog frowned down at the sea as if it was his personal enemy. A cloud passed over the sun and all the brightnesses disappeared at once, leaving the water looking treacherous and cold.

Everyone groaned and started to make their way out of the shelter.

'Come on, come on. Follow me.'

Parry Pysgodyn raced off to gather together the others who were huddled outside the café.

'It's all right for him. Fish like the wet,' I muttered bitterly.

Caradog looked at me. He knew it wasn't the rain that bothered me. It was that my leg was already aching even before tackling the long, steep climb of the road to the camp. It was the thought of everyone jogging off while I trailed behind again. Poor old Cai Cranc, creeping slowly up the hill.

'Tell him you're too tired,' said Caradog. '*Dim problem*. I'll tell him, if you like. He's just in such a rush that he's forgotten about you and your leg.'

I shook my head stubbornly.

'No. It's too embarrassing. He'll tell us to wait here and he'll send the mini-bus out for us like last time. I'll feel a fool.'

'You are a fool.'

Caradog stared at me crossly.

'Look,' I said, 'it'd be like everyone making a big deal each time you went near water. I know I've got a bad leg. You know you're frightened of water. Neither of us want people going on and on about it. It's not exactly *dim problem* but we want it to be.'

I paused for breath. Caradog glowered.

The others were now on the far side of the car park, breaking into a reluctant jog. Parry

Pysgodyn was at the front to encourage them. They were fading away from us as rain turned the village grey. It was no good talking about what we were going to do. It was too late. We were already left behind.

Chapter 10

Caradog walked out of the shelter and stood with his back to me. Rain splashed from the peak of his cap onto his sandals. Rivers of rain ran

down his bare arms and dripped from his elbows. His lilac shorts and lemon T-shirt turned dark as the wet soaked through them. Rain thrummed a staccato beat on the plastic of his lime green backpack.

'Let's go,' he said. 'We'll walk along the beach. It'll be flat for a while and easier for you. Then we'll find a place to climb up to the camp. You'll be rested by then.'

'Parry Pysgodyn said the cliffs are dangerous.'

He had said so but I hated climbing as well. Climbing put a real strain on my leg and I was already exhausted.

Caradog scowled at me.

'What do you suggest then? You've got us into this. Do you want us to get out of it, or not? I can always go to a house and ask them to ring the camp for a mini-bus, if you like.'

He didn't come out with it and call me cowardly Cai Cranc but I felt he wanted to. I was a nuisance. I was hopeless. He didn't like me any more.

'I was thinking of you,' I said sniffily, staring him straight in the eye. 'You won't want to be under the cliffs close to the water. The tide's coming in. You'll be terrified.'

I knew I'd been mean as soon as I'd said it. I was being spiteful—paying him back.

Caradog strode away from me.

'Don't you worry about me. I'm not scared at all. I'm off. *Dim problem.*'

His voice sounded hoarse and different. It shuddered with anger—or something.

'Wait, Caradog. Wait for me!'

I panicked. There was no way I wanted to be left completely alone. Caradog waited impatiently and then we set off across the beach together. Our faces ran with rain. We screwed our eyes up against the blown salt spray of the sea.

It wasn't long before we knew we'd made a bad mistake. The tide had come in further than we'd thought. Once we'd left the main beach, there was little firm, flat sand to walk on. We had to scramble over rocks and wade through trapped pools of water. My leg began to ache more than ever. All the time, the sea sucked hungrily at the shore. Gulped and sucked, gulped and sucked. It made our way forward narrower and narrower. Caradog was silent. He kept his face turned away from the water.

The cliffs rose sheer above us. They looked crumbly, untrustworthy. They were gouged with gullies of loose rock, earth, pebbles, that were always moving, trickling down. The whole world seemed unstable.

The waves kept up a regular, mocking chant that set my nerves on edge.

'We'll never get to the camp this way,' I said at last. 'We'll have to turn back.'

Caradog shook his head and pointed behind us. The sea had already swallowed the way we had come. It now pounded right up against the jutting cliff we'd just passed. It drummed against the foot of the next jagged cliff in front of us. Soon it would cover the seaweed-slick rocks we stood on. The sea had flooded small caves, inlets, at the base of both cliffs. They were full of sea-sound. The caves mouthed the sound back at me—a fearful syllable, dark and dangerous—*cranc, cranc, cranc.*

Chapter 11

'Do you think I could swim for it and get help?' I asked.

Caradog looked appalled and I must admit I didn't fancy my chances. The sea was fish-scale grey, bone white. It churned and spat against the cliffs to each side of us.

'You must be joking! You'd never make it. The currents would smash you into those rocks.'

Waves crashed. Spray lunged, hissed down over rock. The caves mocked us with their deep, yawned echoes.

Caradog was attempting to climb the cliff face. Stones slid beneath his feet as he tried to haul himself upwards, filling his sandals and sending him scrabbling down again. He clutched at tussocks of grass that came away in his hands.

'It's too dangerous,' I told him. 'If you're having trouble down here, think how it'll be at the top. You'd fall and be killed. Besides, you'd never get up there in time before I was drowned.'

We looked at each other. Neither of us had any idea what to do.

'Mmm . . . problem . . .' sighed Caradog helplessly.

The sea sucked towards us. Nearer and nearer. We managed to clamber on to an old rock fall. Caradog climbed first and then pulled me up beside him. There was seaweed on the top and it was slippery, so we knew that we wouldn't be safe for long. Eventually, the water would come up to cover the fall. The sand had already disappeared under the sea. I looked out towards the horizon. There, the surface of the sea rolled and coiled like some restless monster. Its skin slithered, pitted with rain. Once I'd dreamt of

walking out across the ocean but now there was no light on it to tempt or deceive me. It was all depth, darkness, destruction.

My leg throbbed with the effort of keeping my balance on the rock fall. Caradog crouched back against the cliff face. Neither of us spoke any more. Our eyes were fixed on the rise and fall, rise and fall of the waves. Each one came a little nearer, rose a little higher than the last. Nearer and nearer. Higher and higher.

Chapter 12

It was Parry Pysgodyn who came to our rescue. Wyn and Steffan said they'd never seen him flap about so much as when they reached the camp and he discovered that he'd left us behind.

He'd rung the beach café at once and the owner had remembered two boys walking back across the beach and round the headland. Her description of us was spot-on. Even in the rain, my shuffle and Caradog's colours made us stand out. She said she'd been called away to the phone, but had never supposed for a minute that the boys would be daft enough to stay round the headland. Not with the tide coming in.

Parry Pysgodyn had known immediately that Caradog and I would be daft enough.

Wyn and Steffan said they'd never seen him in such a sweat.

'There was old Parry Pysgodyn, oily as a fish, flapping his fins in a panic, eyes goggling, mouth gaping,' they laughed. They did a demonstration together of how he had looked.

It was easy to laugh once we were back. Everyone had laughed. Everyone had cheered.

'Cranc a Cimwch! Cranc a Cimwch!'

The chanting that greeted us was boisterous, excited as a football crowd that was on our side. It sounded nothing at all like the sea.

Parry Pysgodyn grabbed us and hugged us both. We were even more relieved to be back than he was to see us, but being hugged was embarrassing.

'Our courageous crustaceans!' he almost sobbed, trying to make a joke of it.

Caradog rolled his eyes. Siân groaned.

'Oh si—ir!' I said trying to shuffle out of his grasp.

'If we ever get left behind anywhere again,' Caradog said afterwards, 'let me call for a mini-bus or a taxi or even our parents.'

He was right. A mini-bus would have been less embarrassing after all than the lifeboat, and the helicopter, and being hugged by Parry Pysgodyn, and having our picture on the front page of the paper.

The rest of this summer has been the best of times. Caradog and I have seen each other nearly every day, although we've not bothered to visit the beach much. We've both had enough of sea and cliffs for a while. Even the winter might not be so bad when it comes. Caradog is in the football team. He'll have boots and proper kit and training and away matches. I'm in the swimming club now, though, so I'll have *Speedo* trunks and goggles and training and galas. We'll always have time for each other. We'll still be best friends. How could we not be?

Cai and Caradog.

Cranc a Cimwch.

Even our names go together.